Grandma
and the
Rooster

REYCRAFTBOOKS.COM

REYCRAFT BOOKS
55 FIFTH AVENUE
NEW YORK, NY 10003

Reycraft Books is a trade imprint and trademark of Newmark Learning, LLC.

This edition is published by arrangement with China Children's Press & Publication Group, China.
© China Children's Press & Publication Group

Educators and Librarians: Our books may be purchased in bulk for promotional, educational, or business use. Please contact sales@reycraftbooks.com.

This is a work of fiction. Names, characters, places, dialogue, and incidents described are either the product of the author's imagination or are used fictitiously. Any resemblance to actual persons, living or dead, is entirely coincidental.

Library of Congress Control Number: 2020908375

ISBN: 978-1-4788-6973-3

Printed in Dongguan, China. 8557/0121/17583

10 9 8 7 6 5 4 3 2

First Edition Hardcover published by Reycraft Books 2020

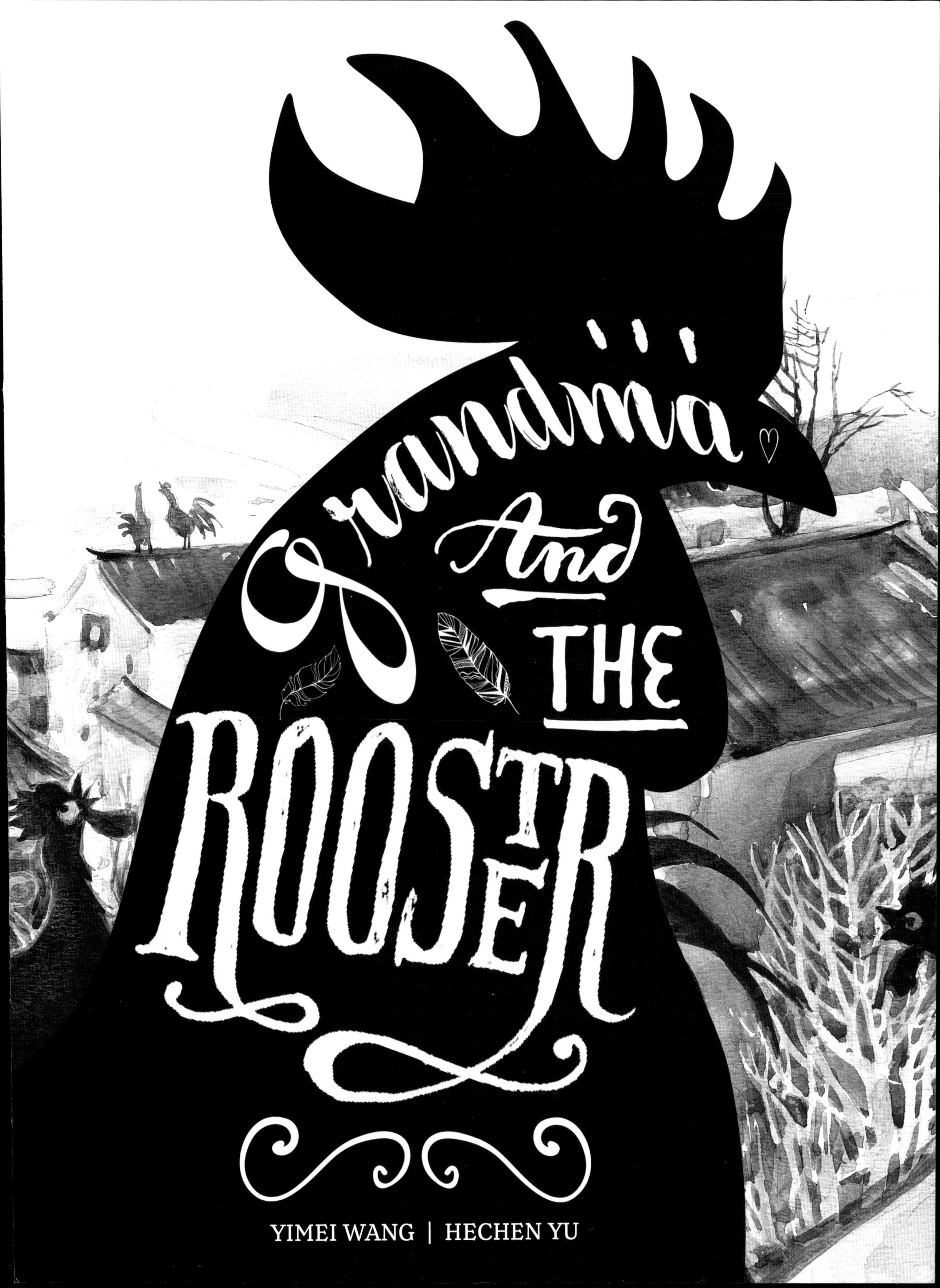

YIMEI WANG | HECHEN YU

"Come down here!"

Grandma called out to her biggest rooster. The bus would be leaving soon, and she was bringing the rooster with her.

This year, for the first time ever, Grandma was not going to celebrate the New Year in her mountain village. Instead, she would travel to be with her family in the big city. She could hardly wait to see her little granddaughter, Xiaoyue.

Grandma planned to
cook her scrumptious
chicken soup for Xiaoyue
to celebrate the whole
family coming together.

The road was crowded with cars and people, all in a hurry to return home for Chu-Xi, Chinese New Year's Eve.

Xiaoyue threw her arms around
Grandma as soon as she arrived. Then
the little girl hugged the big rooster.

"Grandma, I don't want you to make
the chicken soup," she said.

"I want to keep this

rooster!"

"We're not allowed to keep roosters in the city," Dad told Xiaoyue.

"The rooster will crow at daybreak and wake up all the neighbors," added Mom. "And it doesn't smell very good either."

Nevertheless, they decided to keep the rooster.

On New Year's Day, Grandma took
Xiaoyue to visit the neighbors in
their building.

Grandma knocked on the first door.
"Happy New Year to you and your
family! Would it be okay if my
granddaughter keeps this rooster
on the balcony upstairs? I'm afraid
it crows in the morning."

"That would be wonderful!" said the
neighbor, a kind old man. "I usually
wake up to the sound of cars honking.
It's been a long time since I heard
a rooster crowing."

Grandma knocked on another door.

"Happy New Year!"

"I'd like to ask you for a favor. You see, my granddaughter would like to keep this rooster next door . . ."

"Great! I love animals too, as you can see."
The neighbor held out the little dog in her arms.

In fact, everyone in the neighborhood welcomed the rooster. After all, the coming year would be the Year of the Rooster. What better way to celebrate than with a real live rooster?

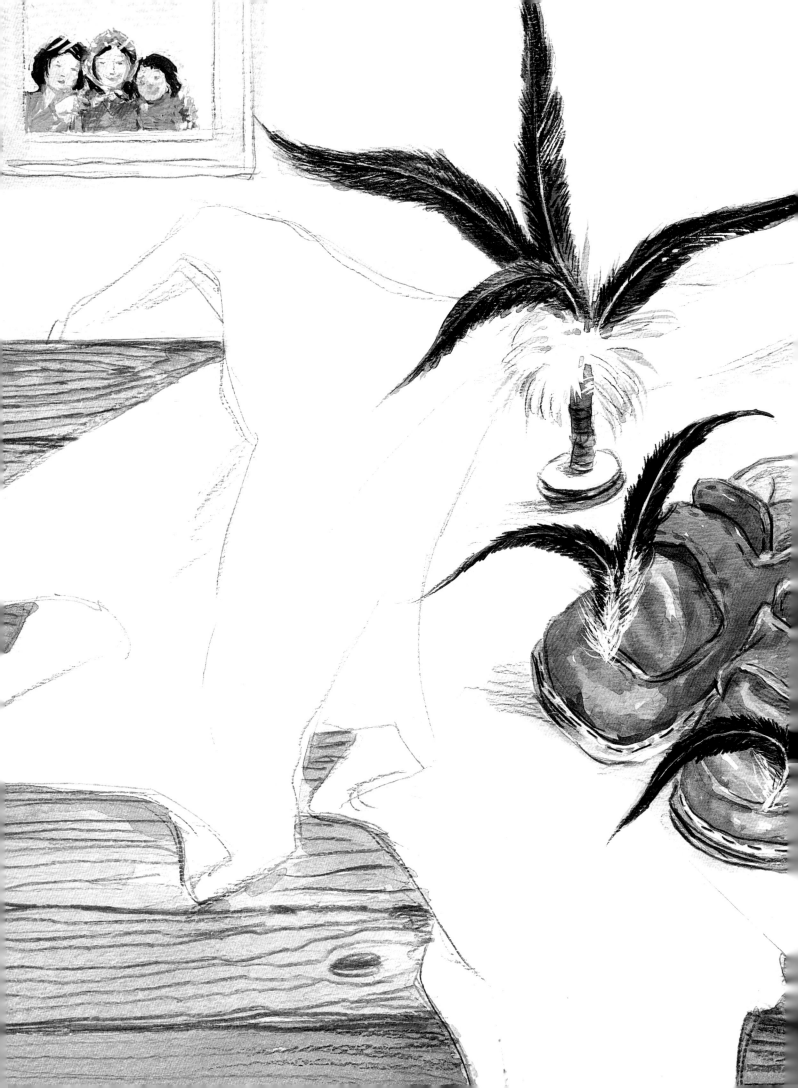

"I have a surprise for you, Xiaoyue,"
said Grandma that afternoon.
"For the Year of the Rooster, I used
rooster feathers to make you a new
pair of cotton shoes and a jianzi."

Xiaoyue was elated!

Xiaoyue put on her new shoes and raced outside to play with the jianzi.

"Look, Grandma!" she cried.

"The feathers shine in the sunlight!"

Grandma and Xiaoyue
went to buy a few treats.
The rooster tagged along, too,
delighting a girl passing by.

"Walking with a rooster in the Year of the Rooster!" she exclaimed.

"But what will you
do when it is the
Year of the Tiger?"

A young man was reading down by the lake.

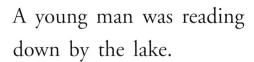

he called out when he saw them stroll by. "You remind me of the rooster I had when I was a boy."

A woman stopped to look at them, too.

"Oh, the New Year has come!" she whispered to herself.

"I would love to go home for a visit with my
mother and her roosters."

Seven days passed and ...

Every morning, the rooster crowed from the balcony.

One day, it even chased after a boy who bullied Xiaoyue.

Reporters came to interview Xiaoyue's family on TV, and the local newspaper published a big article with the headline "Grandma's Gift."

The Evening News

GRANDMA'S GIFT

The young man and the woman who had seen the rooster by the lake both decided to go home to their villages to visit their mothers.

Xiaoyue's kind old neighbor was reminded of the rooster he had as a child. Inspired, he began writing his life story.

Xiaoyue's family all agreed it
had been a wonderful New Year.
But Grandma missed her house
and her chickens. It was time
for her to go home.

Xiaoyue's parents decided that next year they would go to the mountains to celebrate the New Year with Grandma and the rooster. But for now, they all had to say goodbye.

Cock-a-doodle-doo!